The Dirty Cloud Maker

A Journey of Choices

Written and Illustrated

by

Karolee Krause, LPC, SAC

About the Author

Karolee Krause is a Clinical Consultant, Licensed Professional Counselor, Author, and Blogger in the fields of Psychology, Self-Help, and Creative Expression.

Karolee incorporates Narrative Therapy and Storytelling into her clinical work, believing that everyone has a story to tell.

Introduction

The Dirty Cloud Maker is an inspirational story about an angry, troubled character who turns his bad thoughts into dark, dirty clouds and sends them out into the universe where they negatively affect others.

Journey with the Dirty Cloud Maker as he transforms his dark and miserable world into a positive, joy-filled, happy life.

The Dirty Cloud Maker is a reminder of the power of choices, and how each choice, either brings us closer to happiness or leads us deeper into despair.

The Dirty Cloud Maker can be used as a therapeutic tool to address anger, depression and self-esteem issues.

The Dirty Cloud Maker crawled out of his dark and gloomy cave. With his large tattered copper bowl and shiny metal spoon, he gathered blackened stardust that had fallen silently onto the mountain's peak. The stardust was not from bright beautiful stars, but came from dark, moody stars that existed in the furthest and darkest parts of the universe.

Filling his tattered bowl with heavy, dense stardust, he struggled as he made his way back to his lonely cave. Once back inside, he mixed the blackened dust with his own negative thoughts and formed a murky, powdery mix. With each turn of the spoon, the Dirty Cloud maker added in more negativity, anger, hatred, and self-pity.

With one final bad thought
and turn of the spoon, he stood up
and marched out of his cave
carrying his mixture to the most
northern point of the Stellular
Mountain Range.

There he stood in his own darkness and despair, surrounded by silence. Unbeknown to the Dirty Cloud Maker, his own negative thoughts had created his black and darkened world.

Carefully and meticulously, the Dirty Cloud Maker built a fire. With rancid breath, he blew and blew, until the smoke burst into smoldering red flames.

With soot-covered fingers, he took a handful of darkened stardust and threw it into his copper bowl. As the powder hit the flames, it burst into small, dark, dirty clouds that silently floated off into the troubled night sky, dropping particles of anger and hatred along the way.

The Dirty Cloud Maker stood on the edge of the mountain, watching the clouds disappear, thinking bad thoughts about how awful and horrible his life was. He hoped his dirty clouds would rain and storm on others, causing them to suffer as he did.

Meanwhile, in another part of the universe, a village existed where people were living a joyful, happy life. This world was beautiful and clean. Butterflies played in the morning sky and flowers colored the ground. All was well in this village, until one day, a dirty dark cloud appeared in the sky.

MAD
BAD
Thoughts
Toxic
Horrible
hurt
HATE
Alone
No
grim
Fear
Self
SAD
Blame
pity
Awful
Negative

Back on his contaminated mountaintop, the Dirty Cloud Maker kept busy, as he continued to send out negative thoughts in the form of dirty clouds. The darker his mood, the dirtier the clouds became. Covered in filth and grime, he watched as the clouds floated off into the night sky and filtered down into the nearby village.

The villagers went about their days intentionally practicing happiness, until a small child pointed to a single dark cloud that had appeared in the morning sky. They gathered together and watched as the dirty cloud crept along until it stopped directly overhead.

Bad Thoughts
Sad
No one likes me
angry
Help
Leave me alone
fear
You Stink
Go Away
Why me?

As the days passed, clouds clogged the sky above the village. Eventually, the villagers, who had always been kind and caring, became angry and resentful. People shouted at each other and were easily annoyed. No one smiled or laughed. The village filled with garbage, and the soot from the dirty clouds became a reflection of the villagers' own negativity and darkened spirits.

Back on the Stellular Mountain Range, the Dirty Cloud Maker went about his routine, wandering the mountain and collecting the darkest stardust he could find. As his negativity increased, the clouds became larger and dirtier. Still not satisfied, the Dirty Cloud Maker sent the clouds out into the universe and watched as they floated off, feeling a deep emptiness within his soul.

As the Dirty Cloud Maker stood on the mountaintop, he was overwhelmed with emotion. What he didn't realize was that he had created the darkness himself by focusing on the dark stars. In fact, the bright stars were always shining, but his negative thoughts had created his darkened world, and in the darkness, he suffered.

As the dirty clouds continued to accumulate, the villagers' minds became filled with thoughts of selfishness and harm. The Dirty Cloud Maker wasn't happy either. Although he wanted others to suffer as he did, their suffering did not bring him happiness, but only added more to his discontentment.

Then one miserable day, life changed. As the Dirty Cloud Maker came out of his cave to gather stardust, he noticed a single yellow star shining on the mountaintop. The Dirty Cloud Maker had never seen such beauty before. He remained motionless as his anger turned to sadness and his large hollow eyes filled with dark, dusty tears.

The Dirty Cloud Maker felt all of his negative emotions drain from his body. His anger, resentment, self-pity, and hatred began to dissolve. As the sparkling star pierced the darkness of the Dirty Cloud Maker's soul, he realized that it was his dark thinking that had clouded his world and that a beautiful world had always been there. Because of his negativity, he had been unable to see it before.

Suddenly the dark sky dissolved above him, as sunshine lit up the mountaintop, releasing a lifetime of anger, hatred, and negativity. The Dirty Cloud Maker became hopeful for the first time in his life.

Joyful

Hopeful

Playful

Fun

Peaceful

Happy

Laughter

Calm

From that day on, all was well in the Dirty Cloud Maker's life, until he realized that the village was still completely surrounded by darkness. For the first time ever he felt empathy for others. He realized that he had the choice to continue sending dirty clouds out into the universe, or he could begin to make positive new choices.

He now understood that every choice he made not only affected himself but affected others as well. He knew that he had to clear the darkened village of all the dirty clouds.

Life suddenly changed for the Dirty Cloud Maker. He knew that every choice was important, no matter how big or small. With positive thoughts and new energy, he grabbed his copper bowl and shiny metal spoon and scooped up newly fallen, shining stardust that had accumulated on the mountain's peak, and began to create the most beautiful iridescent clouds that he had ever seen.

Happiness
Love
Grateful
Peace
Joy

With good intentions, the Dirty Cloud Maker added in thoughts of love and peace and watched as the clouds sparkled and glistened in the night sky. They floated out into the universe, blessing everyone with the ability to transcend their own dirty clouds.

Goodbye Dirty Clouds!

The End

Made in the USA
Monee, IL
04 November 2023